Holmes Diaries

Sanjay Panikar

Published by Sanjay Panikar, 2022.

This is a work of fiction. Similarities to real people, places, or events are entirely coincidental.

HOLMES DIARIES

First edition. March 20, 2022.

ISBN: 979-8224177875

Written by Sanjay Panikar.

Holmes Diaries

Copyright 2022 Sanjay Panikar
Distributed by Smashwords

Acknowledgements

Numerous people have helped me while writing this book, often without asking and my pleading not to, and always graciously. As I grow older, I am constantly reminded about how many people have been kind and supportive, even though they might privately, have had their misgivings. I would be surprised, if they didn't have any misgivings. I often did. Without their support, often unnoticed and unacknowledged, I would not have been able to publish this book. I am eternally grateful to them. You know who you are.

My thanks to my friend Jonty, who first suggested, I look at putting pen to paper.

Foreword

Holmes is a popular name among archeologists. A small part of the popularity can be attributed to the famous sleuth, Sherlock Holmes, but in most part, its popularity is due to the legendary archeologist Richard Holmes. His successes were many and his failures were much more. He discovered many new civilizations, often at the same site, bewildering most of his fellow archeologists. Luckily for him, he didn't consider scientific proof in high regard and was willing to base his conclusions on feelings.

He had his critics. He had a lot of critics. Just like his, less than high regard for the scientific method, he held these critics in low esteem. He attributed their criticisms to petty jealousies and he never allowed it to interfere with his constant discoveries. He was sought after by many minor regimes all over the world. An archeological excavation by him was bound to discover fascinating and often advanced ancient civilizations in their country. This translated to pride and patriotism for their citizens and vast wealth for the regime heads.

His biggest claim to fame was discovery and deciphering of the Hastinapur civilization. The great Indian epic 'Mahabharat' was based in Hastinapur. Professor Holmes's finding and translation of the sales ledger kept by the tailoring firm Kaurava & Sons, led to a whole new understanding of that ancient civilization. It exposed many myths, and provided an understanding of commerce and professions of some of the main characters in that great epic. The brilliant and widely reported coverage of the discovery and the associated details of the excavation and the method of analysing and deciphering such a huge and rare find, by Mr. Samuel Finch in the Times newspaper, led to Holmes becoming a legend.

There were many firsts credited to this excavation. Before this excavation, radiocarbon dating methods universally relied on Carbon-14, a radioactive isotope of Carbon. But Professor Holmes, an amateur numerologist, reviled the number 14 and instead experimented with other isotopes of Carbon. He finally discovered Carbon-16, a diviner number amenable to more auspicious interpretations. He also wanted to rename Carbon with two C's and spell it as CCarbon. However this proposal was rejected by all and sundry.

He could truly be called the poster boy of the profession. I knew Professor Holmes since he was a young student at The Phoenix Institute. He had joined the institute in the physics department. He was from a small hamlet called Sasabe, located on the border between Arizona and Sonora in Mexico. Both the states claimed Sasabe, as their own. The border literally ran through the hamlet, dissecting his school right at the middle. Depending on where one sat, the language of instruction changed. The teacher's writing across the blackboard often started in one language and ended in another as the chalk crossed the state lines. I have often suspected that Professor Holmes's multifaceted personality was a result of this dichotomous heritage.

He had told me, in a moment of weakness that he was the only literate student in Sasabe at that time. There were other students in his school, but he was the only one who was literate. The other students usually dropped in during lunchtime for the free meals. His teacher had found him a committed (or wanted him committed; the details are sparse) student, given to sudden bouts of intense and silent rumination. His intellect was a matter of speculation. Was he precocious or retarded? Wisely, his parents and others had decided his pensive nature was a sign of precocity, and hence recommended further education for him. In any case, his frequent withdrawal into silent contemplation seemed to have suited, both his teacher and his father. Being poor, his father had to resort to selling parts of his land to finance Professor Holmes's education (the villagers recommendation, was restricted to the question of educating him or not and did not include any financial assistance).

Professor Holmes's choice of particle physics was inspired, as he was not sure, how long he could continue his college education (the land his father owned being finite). Particle physics, being the study of disparate atomic particles (electrons, neutrons, protons, bosons, hadrons, mesons ad infinitum), offered him a chance to harmonise paternal funding with atomic particles. He studied each particle in its entirety before moving to the next particle and managed to reach protons before the land ran out. His education in physics was thus limited at an atomic level due to lack of funds.

A scholarship offered by the archaeology department came to his rescue. At that time, the first two years of the archaeology course consisted solely of practical excavation (theoretical excavation, with simulated digging was added only in the late 1990's). He became passionate about the art and science of digging. For him, the swinging of the hoe was poetry in motion. He acquired one of the most extensive collections of tools and was not averse to displaying them. He developed a nose for the soil. Topography became second nature to him. He could, at a glance, distinguish between igneous and sedimentary rocks. After classes, he practiced in the campus. He perfected the sidearm hoe swing. The university owes him a great debt, as they were able to lay the foundation of the new wing over his trenches. Admittedly, none of the walls are parallel, but this only displays the disdain Professor Holmes held for traditional geometric shapes.

He completed his Bachelors and his Masters in archaeology from The Phoenix Institute. Were it not for the lack of virgin digging grounds, he would have continued on to his PhD. He joined the National Park Services Federal archeology program in 1975 and spent the next few years as an assistant. His superior's appraisals of this period indicate that his assistance, made a big difference, though it is not clear, to what. He improved stratification practices and materials, reworked the sequence of archaeological contexts (within the framework of the Harris matrix). His theoretical work at this time, led to his development of `Law of Continuous Immersion', dealing with the effect of water logging on pre-concrete foundations. He conclusively proved that wood rots in water. During this period, he continued digging with fervour and many of the federal lands bear testimony to his passion. Some metros use his patterns for their pothole design. Many counties covertly appropriate his designs to meet their annual pothole targets. Our magnificently indented roads, despite scientific advances in asphalt materials and road building machinery, are a tribute to Professor Holmes's pioneering work.

In 1985, he left the National Park Service over a minor disagreement on elevation. At one of his sponsored digs, his team dug up one side of the Cahokian mound, leading to the whole structure tilting to one side. He blamed the stratification material. They blamed him.

He returned to the university and was offered the chair (and a desk) of archaeology, which he accepted. He became the chairman of the Society of Archaeologists in 1995 and President of the Digger's association in 1998. He died in his sleep on January 26, 2008, surrounded by his beloved tools!

Professor Holmes kept copious notes and diaries. Many of them are incomprehensible. This book has been gleaned from the ones that are not. In a strict sense, this book is not a biography and there are many gaps in the narrative. The stories are not chronological. The complexity and the sheer haphazard methodology of Professor Holmes's work was a constraint in attempting a chronological book. The stories below are some of the most famous episodes (and the most comprehensible parts of his diaries) in his life. But this episodic arrangement of the chapters merely reflects the life of Professor Holmes, which displayed similar characteristics.

Like his beloved subject of archaeology, Professor Holmes lacked linearity. Many felt, he was an anachronous figure who probably would have been more at home, couple of centuries ago. I have fond memories of the yearly demands he made of his graduate students. The students who remained, till the end, mostly due to lack of imagination and ennui found deeply satisfying alternate employments in the financial sector. Research, if undertaken, has been extensive. I have left no stones unturned, no leads untied to complete the research, if it was done. Wherever possible, cross-references and general explanations have been provided. Factual errors, if any, are inadvertent, but can be fully attributed to the publishers. I strongly urge aspiring students, general readers, amateur enthusiasts and public works officials to grab this book.

Dr. Kevin Hayes, M.A,
    Department of Archaeology
    University of Sonora

Chapter One
Cocoa Forever

When Cambyses wanted to marry his half sister, he was not sure how people would react. Was he half a man to marry half a sister? What about the other half? He asked his council of ministers, who had their heads on their shoulders and preferring it that way, replied with alacrity, that he could. They explained to him, that while the scriptures did not exactly approve of such a marriage, it clearly mentioned that the king could do anything. And he was the king.

Professor Holmes used the above anecdote to explain the dilemma faced by Fernando Cortes when he first met the Aztecs. Professor Holmes had recently come into possession of an obscure supplement to Bernal Castillo's New Spain. The supplement is in a play format consisting of three Acts, with only the second act available. It chronicles the unfortunate meeting between Cortes and Montezuma, the Aztec king. Malinche, Cortes's Mayan friend was also present along with some Aztec and Spanish soldiers.

Cast

Fernando Cortes: the expedition leader and a very bad man

Deigo de Cuéllar: the governor, a less bad man but bad nevertheless

Montezuma: the Aztec king, not bad at all, but prone to melancholy

Tangaxoan: Montezuma's major-domo and a general troublemaker. He fancies Xipaguacin.

Princess Xipaguacin: Montezuma's daughter, a very beautiful narcissistic woman, who admires herself very much.

Malinche: Cortes's Mayan friend (though everyone knew she is his mistress). She also admires herself very much, to everyone else's puzzlement.

La Carvajal: Cortes's favorite trouble-shooter. His preferred weapon was the revolver.

Xever Humberto: a motivated second lieutenant in the army, of royal lineage. He was related to the Catalan Humbertos.

Orlan Reyes: an ordinary soldier in the army of peasant stock. He was related to Miguel Reyes, his father.

The setting is a small hill, surrounded by trees. Cortes is on his horse. Twenty to thirty Spanish soldiers follow him. The soldiers all have muskets and small rocket launchers. There is a small automatic spy drone hovering above, sending live images (no audio) to de Cuellar. Montezuma is sitting on the hill, playing with his many wives and presumably his many children. Few other Aztecs are lazing around. Cortes approaches and shouts:

Cortes: Ola!

Montezuma: Hello!

Cortes: I am Fernando Cortes, the representative of his Highness Alessandro Charles IV, the King of Spain and by royal decree the sole distributor for fine tobacco to the New Colonies. Have you tried some?

Montezuma: No, I prefer local cheroots myself. But I am willing to try the cigarettes. How much do they cost?

Cortes: Ten gold coins.

Montezuma: For cigarettes?

Cortes: No. This is the fee for opening the box containing the cigarettes. You can call it the joining fee. The cigarettes cost 50 gold coins each.

Montezuma: Whew. That is one expensive cigarette. My entire kingdom contains only twenty thousand gold coins. How many cigarettes can I smoke?

There is a flurry of mental activity. La Carjaval puts his hand into his pocket. Everyone becomes tense. He slowly takes out a pocket calculator. Everyone breathes a sigh of relief. He punches in some numbers.

La Carjaval: As per my calculator, you can smoke four hundred cigarettes. At one cigarette per day, you can smoke for four hundred days.

Montezuma: Only four hundred days? What will I do after that? Are you very particular about gold? What about copper? It is also a metal. Less shiny perhaps, but what is there in a shine?

Cortes: Copper! What will I do with copper? His Highness Alessandro Charles has more copper than he can consume. He is now feeding it to his palace servants. They have all become good conductors of electricity. In his palace they stand at the perimeter as an electric fence. No. Copper is of no value. I don't want copper (Cortes sulks and looks away).

Montezuma doesn't know what to do. He wants to know how many cigarettes Cortes has. But the box is locked and the key is with Cortes. He can see the key hanging on Cortes's belt. He calculates his chances of snatching the key. He realizes it is not good and he could get shot. He calculates Tangaxoan's chance of snatching the key. That is also not good, but is more appealing. But before he can execute his plan (and possibly execute Tangaxoan), he decides to negotiate further. He decides he will play along and pay the joining fee.

Montezuma: Can you give me a discount?

Cortes: Yes, we have a special offer for the new customers, Sorry, I meant Colonies. I cannot promise but I will try to waive the joining fees. I will have to check with Highness Alessandro Charles and then confirm. But you have to promise to use at least one hundred and fifty cigarettes in the first six months.

Montezuma: Seems reasonable. But how will I know if Alessandro, sorry, the High Alessandro has agreed to the deal? By the way what is he high on? Can you get some of that stuff for me?

Cortes: You will know it when we submit the bill. In case you do not get the bill due to erratic postal services, you can always call us. I will give you our 24-hour toll free call center number. Do you agree?

Montezuma: Yes.

Cortes calls the helpline number but he is put on hold. He waits. Montezuma waits. All wait. Finally, he gets through, but the agent informs that their systems are down and to try again after a few hours. Cortes doesn't want to wait.

They look for a pigeon to transmit the terms and conditions. They can't find a willing pigeon. The pigeons are afraid of La Carjaval, who has a reputation as a merciless pigeon killer. Finally, a much stronger and braver pigeon is found who agrees to undertake the mission, provided La Carjaval is removed from the vicinity. La Carjaval is persuaded to leave the hill with the promise of an imminent Aztec romp.

Cortes gets down from his horse and walks towards the box. All eyes are transfixed on him. Expectations are high. The crowd is silent. Suddenly, a loud exclamation is heard. It is from La Carjaval, who has just noticed the pigeon's flight. He tries his revolver. He tries the rocket launcher. But the pigeon is smart and swerves from side to side and escapes.

Focus shifts to the box. Cortes opens the box. The cigarettes are beautiful. It is shiny and perfectly crafted. It gleams. It teases. The edges are curved and smooth. Even curvier, and smoother than Xipaguacin. It beckons enticingly, holding hidden promises. Montezuma gestures to one of the soldiers to carry the box to the top of the hill. The box containing one hundred and fifty cigarettes is delivered to Montezuma. His wives and his children crowd around. Except Xipaguacin, who is jealous. They start dreaming. Cortes's party readies to depart, but Malinche is restless.

Malinche: My sweet, handsome and manly Cortes plum! My very own sole distributor to the new colonies! Do you trust Montezuma with these? He has to pay seven thousand gold coins. What if he renegades on the deal?

Cortes: Don't worry Malinche. If he doesn't pay we will send La Carjaval, the pigeon killer.

Malinche: Aah, but I worry. Do you think I should stay back with Montezuma and help him with the cigarettes? This way, I can keep an eye on him? And if I think he is smoking too much, I can step in.

Cortes: Ok. But I think he might not release you later. I will have to entice Montezuma with an exchange offer. What do I have that Montezuma covets?

Cortes decides to ask for Princess Xipaguacin in exchange. A Malinche for a Xipaguacin! What could be fairer than that! This way I get Xipaguacin, who is very young and beautiful, for Malinche, who is old and thinks she is beautiful. Cortes sends Xever Humberto, one of his senior soldiers as an emissary to Montezuma. Xever Humberto is accompanied by Orlan Reyes.

Humberto: Ola! Cortes has asked that Malinche be accommodated with you, in your lofty and beautiful hill till we return. She has tuberculosis, and it is felt that a few months on this lofty hill will help her.

Montezuma: What is this tuberculosis? We do not have this in our world. Oh, what primitive people we are!

Humberto: Your Highness, it is so distressing to know that you do not have this. With Malinche at your side, you will soon have it. Then you and your people can all have tuberculosis.

Orlan Reyes: If she doesn't help, please be assured we will bring some of it with us the next time we are here. But in return Cortes has asked for Princess Xipaguacin. You will agree that it is a small price we are asking. A full community with tuberculosis, for just one princess!

Montezuma: I cannot give Princess Xipaguacin. I cannot live without my beautiful daughter. What about my major-domo Tangaxoan? He is also beautiful from certain angles.

Humberto: All right. Please ask Tangaxoan to pack his bags and come with us.

Xever Humberto, Orlan Reyes and Tangaxoan make their way to the main camp. On seeing them with Tangaxoan, Cortes is livid. He realizes that Montezuma has tricked him.

A Tangaxoan for a Malinche! Nothing could be unfairer than that!

Cortes (angry) to La Carjaval:

Cortes: La Carjaval. What is this I see?

La Carjaval: My Lord. What you see is Tangaxoan.

Cortes: Why do I see Tangaxoan?

La Carjaval: Because Tangaxoan is in front of you.

Cortes: But why do I see him?

La Carjaval: Your Lordship, I will explain. When the light bounces of Tangaxoan and hits the retina of your eyes, it gets converted into electro-chemical signals. These signals travel through your optic nerve and hit the cortex in your brain, which translates this electrical spike as a Tangaxoan.

Cortes looks at the pigeon killer with loathing. He wonders about La Carjaval's cortex. He suspects La Carjaval's cortex may not be entirely in this world, or for that matter, the Old World.

Cortes: You idiot. I am asking why is Tangaxoan here instead of the Princess Xipaguacin?

La Carjaval: Oh I see. Tangaxoan is here with Humberto and Reyes. Maybe he has come to visit us.

Cortes: Shoot him!

La Carjaval: No, my Lord. No. He looks beautiful from certain angles.

Cortes: What are you saying, you psychopathic idiot.

La Carjaval: I am sorry, my lord. I am humbly requesting that we do not shoot him. I suggest we fix him permanently in the angle where he looks beautiful. It will be a beautiful angle.

Cortes: I meant, you moron, shoot Xever Humberto and Orlan Reyes.

La Carjaval: But Xever Humberto is a royal. We can't shoot him. His lineage does not permit it.

Cortes: Really! I am surprised. Can we use the rocket launcher?

La Carjaval: I don't see why not. I am sure we can. The Inquisition Convention says you cannot shoot a royal, but it says you are the Lord of the expedition and the Lord can do anything.

(The reader will note Professor Holmes's reference to Cambyses in this context)

A rocket launcher and revolver kill Xever Humberto and Orlan Reyes respectively, befitting their status. They bury Orlan Reyes. Xever Humberto's mortal remains were not to be found, and hence a decent burial is denied him. Cortes party returns back to Spain.

(The Nahuatl people to this day still speak of a Humberto who floats in the hills and watches over them. He has also become the patron saint of rocket launchers and small missiles: St. Humberto).

Months pass. Malinche, the native Mayan speaker, has now become fluent in Aztec. She has given tuberculosis to Montezuma. Montezuma gave it to his wives. The wives in turn passed it on to their lovers. The Mycobacterium tuberculosis flourished in this new and plentiful land. Soon its mutated varieties, M. bovis and M. africanum joined the fray. Very soon, the community had an abundance of diversified tuberculosis. They had more than they needed.

They wanted to export it but there were no buyers. Montezuma realized the perils of overproduction. The only thing that could reduce the production was the cocoa produced from the humble Cacao tree. This discouraged the mycobacterium from proliferating. Montezuma ordered everyone to drink cocoa from that day on. Since then, every descendant of Montezuma drinks cocoa before retiring for the night. Cortes never returned. He died a rich but unhappy man. Tangaxoan settled in the old world and only spoke with an angle. La Carjaval led a varied and adventurous life. But he continued to kill pigeons mercilessly in his native Iberia. This is why there are no pigeons in Iberia to this day. The bills were never settled and were eventually written off.

Chapter Two
A Bride's Worth

Summers were always a problem for Professor Holmes. It was hot and the searing air hung like a blanket over the campus. There were no impressionable students around to discourse with. There was only an unimpressed Daniel, the department's assistant, a Class IV employee who acted like a Class I employee. Professor Holmes could not discourse with Daniel, since Daniel had a tendency to discourse back.

So, Professor Holmes's afternoons were usually spent lying outside on the bed, and letting his mind wander. But he couldn't allow the mind to wander too far, as it was not safe, especially since a student had been attacked recently in the campus. Thus it was, during one of the safe, proximate wanderings, that the idea of marriage struck Professor Holmes. He tried to strike it back, but it did not budge. He hit his head against the wall to shake it loose, but it refused to leave. Resigned (and bruised), he sat down.

Syllogistic reasoning lead to the realisation that marriage required a bride, of a female gender and persuasion. This ruled out the immediate circle of archaeology students and the faculty. Anatomically speaking, the gender problem could be surmounted, since he was sure some of the students were female (he had checked their application forms). Ascertaining persuasion was a problem. Defeated, resigned (and bruised), he sat further down.

As a professor, he had unlimited access to the university library, constrained only by it being open. Whenever it was open, he could access it. He had recently heard of a wonderful tool, used by many of his more erudite and successful colleagues in the private sector. It was called SWOT. At the library, he found many books on the subject; he took the heaviest one and started his analysis. The reader would be aware, that the first step in SWOT analysis is to state the objective or the desired end state. He took a piece of paper and wrote.

Objective: Woman

Desired End State: Willing

He initially wrote 'Girl' but replaced it later with 'Woman', since he abhorred child marriages. Having thus accomplished the most basic, but usually absent, part of all human endeavours i.e. stating the objective, he felt better. But he knew the objective was too broad and needed to be drilled down (an expression taken from petroleum industry. It provides spatial direction to the crew to avoid upward drilling). Being a man of science and logical reasoning Professor Holmes wrote down his requirements using the Linnaeus method. The following paragraphs are technical, and, therefore, I have taken the liberty to add comments (in brackets) to Professor Holmes's original notes.

Objective: Marriage

Desired State: Willing

Domain: Eukaryota (having complex cells surrounded by membranes for e.g. An iphone in a plastic case)

Kingdom: Animalia (animal like, an attribute popularised in the last few decades of the 20th century)

Phylum: Chordata (a type of stolen data)

Subphylum: Vertebrata (having a spine, but not too much. Hence, it is classified under a sub-section)

Class: Mammalia (having mammaries)

Subclass: Theria (a Hellenised corruption of the word 'tera', as in 'earthly')

Order: Primates (as in ape-like, implying ability to stand upright)

Suborder : Anthropoidea (an idea whose time has gone)

Family : Hominidae (a Hellenised corruption of a minor demon, 'Homini')

Genus : Homo (an androgenised Homini with other preferences)

In short, Professor Holmes realised, he was looking for female person with a plastic covered cell phone containing stolen data; exhibiting child-like animal behaviour having breasts and coming from a demon like family, possessing a male twin with deviant behaviour.

But this didn't sound right to him. He therefore abandoned the Linnaeus method and decided to try an easier method. He understood the power of SWOT analysis and the success of some his classmates in the corporate sector. The next step in SWOT analysis was listing down the internal factors namely his strengths and weaknesses.

Strengths

* a good secure government job with a chair (and a desk) with a good retirement benefits

* Unlimited access to the library

* University provided accommodation including hot water supply

* flexible and limited phenotypic requirements in the bride. Any regular polygon would suffice.

* a silver credit card with unlimited spending limit as per the bank (though he suspected this to be not true)

* a keen intellect, ready and willing. A less keen body, hopeful and very willing.

* a fine collection of digging tools

* Computer

Weaknesses

* lack of a better job

* lack of a Gold credit card

* uncooperative faculty, subject to constant infighting

* Daniel

* Computer

The listing of the computer in both the sections, though rare was not uncommon. In this case, he had listed it, due to the department's inability to use it. It had arrived without the power cable and possibly many other cables, but the faculty, being technically challenged was unable to get it working. They had tried everything including praying, cajoling and finally kicking, but to no avail.

Professor Holmes had a more difficult time completing the external factors of the SWOT analysis. He couldn't see any opportunities and other than getting rid of Daniel. He couldn't see any threats. He knew he would have to make some changes to keep his wife happy. It would be inconvenient but not a threat.

Thus with an incomplete analysis and a much simplified objective, Professor Holmes turned to the task of acquiring a bride. As an archaeologist he was aware of the 'clubbing method' (a popular method in ancient tribes where potential brides were hit on the head with a club. This usually solemnised the marriage, unless someone with a bigger club turned up and hit the potential bride again. In which case it was followed by a joyous (not for the bride), marriage or a burial.

Times had changed and anyway he didn't have a club and didn't know anybody who had a club. He needed an alternative tool to solemnise the marriage. He considered the long iron flagpole, in front of the building, but he discarded the idea, as it was too long (he would have to ask the applicant to stand still at least 30 feet away, while he tried hitting her head). He realised he needed outside help. Since other than himself, the only person presently available was Daniel, he asked Daniel. He asked for coffee and advice. He was advised not to ask for coffee.

He decided to place a classified advertisement. It ran in the February 18, society edition. He got many responses (including one from Tam Wo of Seoul, Korea). Some didn't have phones, most didn't have 5G connections, and all didn't have stolen data. Some had enclosed their photo. The shyer ones had enclosed only the photo frames. Both were not to his taste.

It was at this juncture, that Professor Holmes approached me for assistance. After reviewing the case it was clear to me that Daniel's advise to not ask for coffee might be symptomatic of a deeper problem. He might be more amenable to being undisturbed. With this acute observation dispensed with, I turned to the problem of finding a bride. My initial suggestion of replacing the bride with a more readily available bridegroom was overruled. I agreed with Professor Holmes that finding a suitable club was difficult and in high probability, illegal, and in any case the clubbing method was passé.

The flagpole with its current dimensions would lead to an issue of manoeuvrability (of the rod and not the potential bride. It was assumed the bride would be willing to stand still). I suggested cutting it into a more manageable length. He was not keen and wanted to avoid any premarital physical work altogether.

He preferred to be an armchair suitor. With this new condition imposed, I suggested one of the dating websites. It boasted of a million users. Based on the last census' male-to-female ratio, we arrived at a potential pool of 380,000 registered female users. Using a combination of regression analysis, binomial theorem and mostly imaginary numbers (a very useful numeric system developed by Gerolamo Cardano, later appropriated and used extensively in Wall Street) completed, we were beginning to feel we had made progress. We knew what we wanted; we knew what our chances were. Extending the above ratio to the country's total female population, we derived a potential set of half a million eligible brides. Arizona alone had more than 3.8 million females. Therefore, every seventh female in Arizona was a potential bride. I suggested looking at California in addition to Arizona. But Professor Holmes turned this down, as he didn't agree with the climate change theories being embraced by them.

Still, this was very easy. Science had triumphed again. A bride was worth 7.6.

However, as an epilogue, Professor Holmes's search for a bride was not successful. He couldn't resolve the fractional value prescribed by the analysis. He kept looking intensely at every 7.6th woman he met, but they were fragmented and his search remained fruitless. I realise now in retrospect, that fractions were not his forte.

He remained a bachelor till the end.

Chapter Three
Mahabharat Revisited

The recent excavations in northwestern India by Professor Holmes have introduced new evidence about the Indian epic. It turns out that the narrative is more prosaic and mundane than is commonly believed, though there are moments of sheer brilliance. Its monotonous vapidity interspersed with occasional profound insights into the human condition remains a fathomless mystery into the main characters of the epic. Who were they, and why did they behave the way they did?

It did not help that a research paper titled, 'Social Dynamics and Influence of Melodrama on the Hastinapur Sun Dynasty' was published anonymously a few weeks before the excavations started at the site. Whispers of subterfuge and hyperbole have surrounded Professor Holmes's team since then. The first breakthrough came when one of the junior archaeologists accidentally tripped and fell down into a hole. Being a junior archeologist this was ignored. Repeated moans and pleas from the hole led to a closer scrutiny. The reason for the fall was found to be a metal plate sticking out of the ground. The fall, which later came to be described as the 'Junior Fall', was helped by the fact that the archaeologist was helplessly inebriated at the time. The metal plate was dug out carefully and the archaeologist buried in its place.

The first thing the Professor Holmes's team did was to analyse the age of the plate. A proprietary atomic dating technique developed by Archaeology Institute (AI) was used for the dating. The analysis concluded that the plate was probably anywhere between 75 years to 45 million years old. Next, the plate was cleaned thoroughly. Professor Holmes's team, painstakingly, and in some cases, without pain, cleaned the plate. The job was laborious and took the team a full six years to complete. In a later and more candid interview, Professor Holmes admitted that the job could have been completed in two months. But as he was seven years from retirement, and the weather was pleasant, it was decided to complete the job in six years.

The plate was found to be a signboard painted in the classical Red Claypot method. It was written in the traditional language of the period, which has not been deciphered so far. Fortunately, the sign contained other clues and Professor Holmes using his now famous 'Gut Feelings' method deciphered it. The plate read 'Kaurava & 100 Sons, Tailors to the King'. Beneath that, it contained in smaller letters, the tagline 'We also undertake all kinds of ladies stitching'.

This discovery has thrown new light into the whole meaning of the epic. It is clear that sartorial sense was highly developed during those times (anywhere between 75 years to 45 million years old). The whole economic and social fabric was founded on it. In those times, most of the people died of starvation and the rest were killed due to their dressing style. Style statements were highly ritualistic and had rigid structures. This discovery has required us to revisit certain incidents in the story.

When, in Chapter Eight of the Mahabharat, Lord Krishna says to Arjuna: "You are worried, my friend about the cut of your clothes and you say to yourself; Does clothes maketh a man?" This, when looked at closely, helps us in understanding Arjuna's fascination with his appearance and provides insight into his bravado in the battlefield. Arjuna was following a simple mathematical logic; if you are the only one left alive, then by deduction and common sense you are the best dressed. The further implication of this was the discovery of the management strategy known as the 'zero sum game'. The Chinese due to absence of similar phonetic sounds call it the 'dim sum game'

The Annual report and the accounting entries of 'Kaurava & 100 Sons, Tailors to the King' found beside the plate, also throws light on the famous scene where Draupadi, a famous queen is unceremoniously, and some say, lecherously undressed. It is not what we had previously believed. It was a test fitting, the kind that has gained popularity in the last 50 years. Since Draupadi was a queen, she had the financial resources to order the latest designs from the distant city of Parsipur. Unfortunately, the dress did not fit properly and the best tailors from 'Kaurava & Sons, Tailors to King' were called in to help.

The fitting was in the presence of her inner courtiers, and we have no reason to believe any unbecoming behaviour was displayed. Unfortunately, the King, who immediately took umbrage at the activity, interrupted it. This unwarranted rudeness and subsequent thrashing of the innocent fitters led to a great rift between the two groups.

This misunderstanding could be ascribed as the casus belli for the Great War. Clearly, it is the greatness of our epics that such stories continue to hold meaning and provide answers even after many centuries. The inner significance has not changed even after 75 years to 45 million years. Evidently, the great saints and seers had the vision and the wisdom, to list down the main problems facing humanity. Does the red tie go better with the blue shirt or the red shirt? Is a brown belt acceptable with a black shoe?

Answers to such profound questions remain unanswered; and as the dig progresses we hope that Professor Holmes and his team will provide us further answers.

(This story was first published by Mr. Samuel Finch in the Times newspaper. Reprinted with permission)

Chapter Four
The New Bling Dynasty

In June 1999, I was invited by, the Dean of University of Chowho, for participating in a local archaeological excavation. They had unearthed a large diamond tiara, with the maille work containing a weave technique never seen before. He invited me, since my earlier work on the Carcanet's worn by the Bhillas tribe in the 2nd century CE had given me a minor reputation as an expert on the Carcanet's worn by the Bhillas tribe.

I was excited but a bit worried. University of Chowho worked under a communist doctrine. Their expertise in archaeology was limited, since they refused to study any laissez faire civilisations. This had limited their scope to human societies from the early 20th century onwards. In absence of ancient civilisations, post 1917, they had not been able to undertake any serious fieldwork. In addition, the region was undergoing a change. The glacial waters particularly suited for poppy cultivation was melting. From the biggest consumer of opium, they had become the biggest exporter of refrigerators. But the refrigerators were not edible, and did not take you to the places, that opium could. Hence the local travel industry was in recession. The land, rich in minerals like lead and melamine, was getting depleted.

Basic rights were improving, though farm animals still could not vote. The secret service gave their reasons before they shot you. Taking comfort in the improving situation, I accepted their request. To familiarise myself with the case, I requested the Dean to send me the diamond. He refused.

In exasperation I asked for the details of the dig. He sent me the following synopsis: 'A peasant found a big diamond tiara in his field. He was shot. Dead. We think it is from a new dynasty: the Tiara, not the peasant. It could precede or succeed the Ming dynasty. Peasant uncooperative and not speaking'. This was perplexing and possibly big.

The peasant held the clue. But what was the clue? And why was he uncooperative? Was he hiding something? Clearly, he was shot before the shooter had heard of the improving human rights situation. I knew a new dynasty would be great find. I had always felt that the transition from Yuan dynasty to Ming dynasty to Qing dynasty was not as smooth as believed. Phonetically speaking, why an 'M' after 'Y'. And where did 'Q' fit in? If it was a 'U', it could be an anagram of 'YUM'. But what does 'YUM' mean? Could it be the now lost incantation used in making noodles? Or was it the Malaysian's articulation of the letter 'M'? If so, it could explain the similarity between Malaysian Mee noodles and Chinese noodles, strengthening the theory of early culinary trade between the civilisations. Such thoughts began to occupy my mind. Admittedly, without any basis I started wondering if this new dynasty was the speculated 'Uing dynasty', the missing link in completing the anagram. I realised this investigation required an expertise that I was not sure, I had. I realised I needed Professor Holmes's help. But would he oblige, since he was still struggling with fractions. But he owed me, for my help in resolving the SWOT analysis (refer A Bride's Worth for details) and I knew he would not be able to resist a challenge of this magnitude. We both arrived in Chowho in July. We were eager to start our research and proceeded to the dig immediately. The field was covered with refrigerators till the eye could see; of all sizes and colours.

We arrived at the place where the tiara was found. The university students had placed the dead peasant on the spot to mark the location. The shooter was placed nearby to ensure the peasant stayed. We wanted to shift the peasant, but the shooter signalled his disagreement by taking aim at us. The Dean had to intervene and after explaining the improvement in human rights, the shooter allowed us to proceed, provided the peasant stayed in his place. We started digging underneath the peasant. But the work was slow, hampered frequently by the peasant falling in. Despite this, we made progress. Professor Holmes took the first turn with the grub hoe. At two feet, he struck the peasant (who had fallen in). At three feet, he struck gold, or rather, a gold brooch. We were thrilled (except the peasant who remained expressionless). I grabbed the hoe from Professor Holmes and started digging (after striking the peasant, for luck) feverishly. At four feet, I struck gold again; this time it was a necklace showing the same maille pattern. It was getting late and we retired to the camp leaving the shooter to keep the peasant company. We took stock. We had found a diamond tiara, a gold brooch and a gold necklace. Though we had not dated it yet, the casting and soldering method used, indicated an era of great ostentation and pretension. These people believed in glamour, and the segmented nature of their society was evident from the correlation of the find and its depth. In honour of these insights, we named the dynasty as the 'Bling Dynasty'.

The dating of the artefacts needed to be completed. The methodology had to be finalised: Carbon-14 or the AI method. Carbon-14 was more precise, but the AI method was more amenable to budget allocations. The calendar system needed to be finalized; the choice being a capitalistic Gregorian calendar, or the traditional Xia calendar; or the more proletarian Solar Gulag calendar (based on the number of summers spent at the labour camp). After much democratic discussion, it was decided to use Carbon-14 in a Gregorian setting.

The results were not as expected. Carbon-14 analysis indicated the artefacts were very recent. The Bling dynasty was a recent phenomenon. The Dean was happy. This ensured continuation of the excavation. The peasant remained expressionless. Professor Holmes and I were unhappy. The anagram was incomplete. The Malaysian Mee was not the template for noodles. They were independent developments.

Postscript: Being recent, the period was renamed the 'New Bling Dynasty'. University of Chowho continued their excavations till the peasant finally disintegrated. The work has halted. They are awaiting a replacement peasant to shoot and resume work. They have already discovered many shiny artefacts. We hope they discover more.

Chapter Five
Two Fainting Goats

Professor Holmes's excavations in the northwest, led to the discovery of the ancient civilisation of Histrionia along with their myths relating to the creation of the world. Carbon-14 dating has placed the civilisation between 3700 and 4000 years old. But this was found to be too precise for the archaeological fraternity, leading to stifling of further investigations and consequently a reduction in their expense budgets. Using the proprietary dating technique developed by AI during the Mahabharat excavation, it was conclusively proven that the Histrionic civilisation existed in the Past. Using credit scoring templates, where past history is crucial, it was also conclusively proven that the study of Histrionic civilisation was necessary and needed additional funding.

The best preserved of the documents found at the site is the 'Two Fainting Goats' scroll. Using a combination of diluted sulphuric acid, naphthalene and the services of the local laundry, Professor Holmes managed to clean parts of the scroll. Depending on funding and cash infusions, the complete work is expected to be completed within this decade. The cleaning process was intensive. The scroll was placed in a diluted sulphuric acid bath for a day and then dried. Powdered naphthalene was sprinkled over it to avoid insect infestation. This process managed to remove all of the soil and most of the fabric from the scroll. All that remained are a few threads of pristine white colour. Over a period of a few weeks, Professor Holmes studied the white threads from all the sides and managed to conclusively confirm it as the 'Two Fainting Goats' scroll.

But the scroll has been a subject of controversy ever since it was found. A section of the archaeologists believe it should be read as 'Two Fatherly Gods' scroll. They base their claim on the fact that the scroll relates to the creation of the world, and by association a divine hand, or in this case, a set of hands, could be involved. The writing is a combination of vers libre and tercet. Its narrative style is complex, with an exalting diction. It is estimated to contain 24 chapters of 10 stanzas each. This is a very rough estimate, as the scroll has not been completely restored. Professor Holmes has based the estimate using a simple calculation of the string and stanza lengths. The font seems to be a Sans Serif font. Their use of Sans Serif font might indicate the Histronite's difficulty in complicating things. The curls and feet required for a Serif font, was perhaps, beyond their simple imaginations. There are many repetitive verses, and it is believed that this style of repetition of the same thing over and over again, is the basis of the modern day histrionics, often manifested among our people. The original verse (in Roman script) and Professor Holmes's translation is reproduced below:

Chapter 1

Stanza 1

Iouweriou iwqeioroi Akklasior

Lkjkgjd kljfdl Akklasior Klreuwpmcd

Oooooh, Aaaaaaaa, Ooooooooooh

Translation:

In the beginning was the Goat.

Before the Goat, was void

Oooooh, Aaaaaaaa, Ooooooooooh

The scroll is not clear on the status of the universe before the void. Were there multiple voids, signalling the existence of multiple universes? Or was there A Void? The second option seems probable i.e. A void (or Avoid in popular usage).

Stanza 2

Sdfkl lfiok Akklasior

Lkjkgjd kljfdl Klreuwpmcd

Oooooh Akklasior, Aaaaaaaa Akklasior, Ooooooooooh

Akklasior

Translation:

The Goat was a wonderful Goat.

He was the pinnacle of Goatdom.

Oooooh Goat, Aaaaaaaa Goat, Oooooooooooh Goat.

This stanza gives us our second clue on the Histrionic word for a male Goat. It was 'Akklasior'. It is also the first indication of the illogical basis of the histrionic narrative style. We have been told, only about the Void and the Goat? How could the Goat be the pinnacle of Goatdom? The traditional definition of the word 'void' is nothingness or emptiness. We are left with 'nothingness' and a 'goat'. In such a state of the universe, it was highly dramatic and irresponsible of the practitioner of histrionics to uphold the Goat's attributes as a pinnacle. Professor Holmes believes this is an early example of the 'bizarre absolute' pathos practiced among histrionic people even today.

Stanza 3

Akklasior jkiwepp Klreuwpmcd

Klreuwpmcd jkiwepped ujio. Rfe Akklasior not kuiol.

Oooooh yupa Klreuwpmcd , Aaaaaaaa yupa Klreuwpmcd ,

Oooooooooooh yupa Klreuwpmcd

Translation:

The Goat looked at the Void.

And the Void looked back. And The Goat was not happy.

Oooooh Bad Void, Aaaaaaaa Bad Void, Oooooooooooh Bad Void

While the second stanza was considered inappropriate and probably a later addition, it is in the third stanza that the real depth of their creation myth starts manifesting. The narrative becomes more poignant and philosophical. The Goat's looking at the Void is a metaphor of the common human condition of staring at nothing. We stare, but we see nothing. Objects, sights, colours, smells merge into a unified mass of transparent ether. Interestingly their observation about the Void staring back shows their deification of 'Nothingness'. Nothing was divine, in their belief system.

The third sentence introduces the concept of happiness. This introduction, so early in the narrative, showed that these people were in a hurry. But hurry to do what? Why didn't they wait for a few more stanzas of metaphysical musings before introducing this elusive conceptual emotional state? Did the composer have other plans? Perhaps, he had in mind a weekend sojourn? Or could it be another scroll to be filed before the deadline? We don't know!

Stanza 4

Akklasior mnbfklwe, io tyukil roem

Io tyukil bhukml, tyukil zswdrf, tyukil vfexft

Okm thiw uythr ajkui Io tyukil erend Akklasior!

Translation:

The Goat sulked mightily. He wanted more.

He wanted a house, he wanted a car, and he wanted

multiple loans.

But, most of all, he wanted another Goat!

The fourth stanza continues on the same theme of temporal desires. While the third stanza introduces the end state briefly, the fourth stanza provides us with more specific clues. Dr. Hardik et al, have called the fourth stanza as the most important section in the scroll as it demonstrates the worldly desires of the histrionic. The phrase 'wanted more' in the first line illustrates their knowledge of comparative dimensions. They seem to have had an understanding of relative measures. The second line is a matter of dispute. The specificity shown is very rare in texts of this period and some believe it to be a later addition. Similar creation texts usually use more abstract terminology like dwellings, camels and gold. The third line indicates the basic human desire of the pastoral histrionic people i.e. a goat. It was a source of milk, food, clothing, and for the more flexible and undiscerning pastoral males, a satisfier of the most basic human need.

Stanza 5
Rtgh Lo Hejino! Yokiuo erend Okklasior
Powler Okklasior , Akklasior lupista. Powler Akklasior
lupis, Okklasior lupista.
Oooooh wer lupista Kklasior, Aaaaaaaa wer lupista
Kklasior, Oooooh wer lupista Kklasior
Translation:
And Lo Behold, there was another female Goat
Seeing Okklasior, Akklasior fainted. Seeing Akklasior faint,
Okklasior fainted.
Oooooh Two fainted Goats, Aaaaaaaa Two fainted Goats,
Oooooh Two fainted Goats

Stanza five introduces the female goat for the first time in the narrative. The histrionic word for a female Goat was 'Okklasior'. The text is not clear on why Akklasior fainted. Was Okklasior not of goat like proportions? Was she not introduced properly? Maybe Okklasior did not conform to the definition of classical goat beauty. And if not, why not? It raises (apparently, not for Akklasior) many philosophical questions. In a Two Goat world, who is the beauty and who is the beast?

Professor Holmes has been able to complete the translation only till the fifth stanza. Clearly, the world of the histrionics was complex and Professor Holmes's task in deciphering the scrolls is a big challenge. The theme deals with many complicated elements. There are very few references available and other creation texts of the same time period do not display similar complexity and depth. What happened to the histrionics? Where did they go? One theory, holds that they intermingled with other neighbouring tribes and eventually disappeared altogether. Today, they occasionally show up in our midst. As the scrolls are translated, we can expect further glimpses into the daily life of the Histrionics and to the fantastic tale of Akklasior and Okklasior.

Chapter Six
The Silicon-Based Life

To people who didn't know him well, Professor Holmes was a polymath, a true savant, a tireless harvester of knowledge. (to people who knew him well, he was just tiresome). His interests were eclectic and spanned a broad range of subjects like economics, paleontology, social anthropology, aerobics (as a spectator), mathematics, architecture and herbal medicine.

But among the varied subjects he dabbled in, evolutionary biology was his foremost passion. He strongly believed in evolution and did not believe in traditional creationism (though he privately believed some of his colleague's antecedents and evolutionary progress was not smooth, and may have been outcomes of punctuated creationism. Unfortunately, time did not permit him to fully develop his theory of punctuated creationism). In evolution, he leaned towards the quantum evolutionists and disdained phyletic gradualism.

I am explaining this in detail, so that the readers can understand the context of his research. The reader may find some of his notes naive and ingenuous, but this can be attributed to his environment during his formative years. I was delighted to receive an invitation from Professor Holmes to join him in his research at New York, which is in America. I had heard of New York and knew that anything with a 'New' in its name would be interesting. In the middle of the city in a place they call Wall Street, they had discovered a new form of life. It was called Wall Street, as the inhabitants there had a big wall running around the settlement. It is unclear if the wall was to keep the other humans and animals out or to keep the inhabitants in. Though the evidence for a new form of life was meagre and based on very few samples, it was nevertheless strange. If proven correct, it would have strengthened Professor Holmes's theory of punctuated creationism. On the few subjects studied, the chromosomal mapping showed a major shift in gene structure and cell composition. In these individuals, while normal RNA, DNA, amino acids and enzyme activity existed, certain parts of their cellular metabolism had shifted from carbon based to silicon based.

It also led to a possible reopening of the Lamarckian argument, since clearly these individuals, had at birth, been carbon based, but during their professional life had acquired other chemical characteristics. Thanks to Professor Holmes's reputation as an imaginative thinker who could leap vast expanses of logic and reasoning effortlessly to arrive at simple conclusions, he was offered by a local think tank (to our readers who are less globalised, it is a group of thinkers who are paid well) to write a futuristic paper on the evolution of this sub species.

Professor Holmes could not complete the paper, due to the unavailability of think tank's promised money. However, I was lucky to get his notes. His notes seem to have been written, as and when thoughts struck him. I have attempted to think through (with moderate success, as I didn't have a tank) his ideas and have endeavoured to present them to you in plain non-scientific language. I have notated the silicon-based life forms as bankers as most of the subjects are from this profession.

March 6: The silicon seems to have seeped in from the numerous computers, cables and networks surrounding their living space. The computers seem to have been manufactured in many sizes, with the most prevalent being the size of a small bag, which is carried across the shoulder. In fact, Professor Higgins, who is the main project director of the study, believes this bag contained the brains of these people. They also use a smaller machine frequently, called the 'PDA'. It seems these were used for making decisions of lesser importance. They seem to have used their biological brains sparingly for few hours a day. The rest of the time was quite brain free.

March 7: Explore the possibility of these people using the computer as a fighting tool! This is an interesting hypothesis. My rudimentary tests (I threw the computer at a person who had come to visit Professor

Higgins) indicate that it would have been difficult to throw these at the enemy due to its weight. And as a piercing instrument it would have been pointless, as it did not have any point. Another possible explanation is that they used these machines as a visual weapon, to mesmerise the carbon-based people by displaying colourful graphical images and numerical texts. Once they were under this state, the bankers could get them to do their bidding. If this failed, perhaps they hit the carbon-based people on their heads with their lighter PDA.

March 9: I have done a complete survey of the area. These people really love signboards and at night seem to function completely under multi-coloured lights. What a contrast to my village where we had one lamp, which was shared by all the 40 families. We had to wait for 40 days for our turn to get the lamp. My half brother and me (he was only half my size) would spend hours staring at the lamp, in darkness, till it was time to return it to the village headman next morning. Most of the signboards have the word 'bank' in them. They clearly love to express their difference from other carbon-based life forms. Some of them have the word 'sleeps'. Not being familiar with their social structure, can only lead to the guess that these people sleep a lot. Perhaps their inorganic brains were connected to the network during these hours and substituted routine mental activity; to be explored further!

The next entry is dated a few days later. During this period, Professor Holmes became enamoured with the reception girl at his hotel. The enamouring was entirely one sided. She reminded Professor Holmes of one of the girls at his village (with long black hair till her hips and strong thick legs till the ground). Unfortunately, she had been the headman's daughter and any dalliance had risked losing the lamp privileges. Luckily for us, this break enthused Professor Holmes to study the philosophical and metaphysical aspects of these subjects.

March 17: They are an advanced people with clear understanding of the metaphysical world. They have developed ephemeral tools called CDOs, CDS, among others. These tools seemed to have been sold to each other till the tool evaporated. On evaporation, they would make another one and start selling again to each other. Based on how many they sold in a year, they were paid. Their silicon brains were designed in such a way that they just needed to type the buyer's name and a complex algorithm would fill in the rest. Their brains were really powerful. To make these complex algorithms, they employed a set of external people (their cellular structure needs to be studied further). These external people are a very creative lot and spend many hours creating advanced realities. Their reality business is very advanced, indeed. They also make graphical images to mesmerise the bankers. If this failed, perhaps they also used their PDAs for more physical convincing (called buy-in in their vernacular). Their PDAs are bigger and sturdier. My experience indicates an inherent danger in these buy-in exercises. But it may be detrimental to kill the non-buyed-ins (related to the bedouins, a fiercely independent tribal people in Arabia who rarely buy-in). Whatever the method might be, clearly the route taken by the vector to gain admission is the Power Point, a very powerful pointed tool.

March 19: They had intensive interactions with the carbon-based people across the wall. For trading they used something they called 'Loans'. Some of the documents especially during the later period refer to these as 'Sub-prime Loans'. It is not clear what caused this change. It may be in honour of their ruler who was sub-prime. It is etymologically linked to the word 'Sublime' and their ruler may have been sublime. These 'Loans' were sophisticated instruments and were given to anyone regardless of caste, creed, profession, income or religious persuasion (a truly egalitarian process to be adopted more vigorously among our people). People used these instruments to buy houses, cars and household appliances. It is not clear how the bankers benefited from these. One theory being considered is they were paid, based on the quantity of these 'Loans' they disbursed. Once people used these for houses and cars they discarded it or returned it to the bankers. This was called repossession in their language. Clearly, they do not believe in wasting anything. They are the world's first environmentalists. All their goods and services were sold and repossessed and then sold again, till like the CDx's they evaporated and vanished.

March 20: Being a Sunday, I am not able to think. Am I getting too influenced by the subjects? I wish I had access to the think tank.

March 21: Thinking again! Was lucky to find a piece of paper called a `Memo'. It provided big clues into their social structure. Undoubtedly, a very rigid caste structure divided into four broad categories. The first three are what they call management and all metaphysical idealisation was restricted to them. The fourth group did all the work. To explore further: the similarity to the 4th century BCE Akkadian civilisation! These memos seem to be a communication medium. Independent thought is discouraged and it seems these memos serve as the standard homogenised thinking template.

March 23: Their PDAs, or the little brain, provides many clues to the daily life of these people. One of their major activities seemed to be called `meetings'. The inhabitants were exceedingly fond of `meetings'. Many of these `meetings' were written down in something called `minutes'. Was it called `hours' if it exceeded sixty minutes? I suspect these gatherings are their way of appeasing their gods and may have been a form of divine worship. They usually gather in a circle except when a member from the higher caste was present. Then the preferred shape was a rectangle. Their buildings contain many such places of worship, varying from the small to the really big and ostentatious. Before they undertook any activity the inhabitants would hold a `meeting'. Depending upon the gravity of their undertaking, and its impact on their economic well-being, they might hold multiple `meetings'. Social rank in their society was also based on how many `meetings' an individual attended. The upper strata of their society lived purely on `meetings'. They would congregate in a central area (called the meeting room) and conduct their religious chanting. Evidence indicates that most of them were well versed with the chants, since they did not take their big and little brains to the room. Clearly, such religious activity was a main component of their daily life.

March 25: Time is running out. Professor Higgins is becoming uncooperative. He visited me at the hotel again. I saw him smiling at the girl at the reception. Why? Shouldn't the guest have the first right to smile?

March 30: Cannot concentrate! Have decided to discontinue the research. Will give my notes to Dr. Higgins. The notes end abruptly. Was the lack of access to the tank hampering progress? Was he finding it difficult to reconcile to Professor Higgin's interest in the receptionist? Was Professor Holmes's yearning for the headman's daughter interfering with his concentration? The notes do not provide a clue. Many months later I had asked Professor Holmes about his reason for giving up the research. He did not reply. He said it gave him nightmares and he was frightened.

Chapter Seven
Hypatia's Murder

Professor Holmes's interest in mathematics and geometry led him to conduct private research into the life of Hypatia. It was the summer break and he was relatively free from his academic obligations at the university.

Hypatia belonged to the second Alexandrian school, which was preceded by the first Alexandrian school, around the 3rd century CE. The school had been undergoing a period of turbulence due to the loss of political independence and absorption into the Roman Empire, which in turn was in transition from a Republic to an Empire. However, there is no proof of mistreatment under the new masters, other than the placement of a contingent of Roman infantry near the gates. Students continued to flock to the Alexandrian school, but had to undergo stringent security checks. Mathematicians like Euclid, Archimedes and Apollonius of the first school were still influential, though their factual theorems were losing popularity.

Planetary mechanics had fallen into a rut, chord dynamics was falling into one and the Screw already perfected by Archimedes, had lost its charm (for disambiguation, not to be confused with the current usage of the word as a verb, which remains charming). Only Euclid's Mule observation† remained unanswered (continues to vex to this day). All other mysteries had already been solved or so it seemed. It was in such a hopeless mathematical landscape, that Hypatia was born. We know her father was Theon. We know her mother was Theon's wife. We know this from references in Ptolemy's Almagest, which says 'mother of Hypatia was a woman and she was Theon's woman'.

Hypatia was born in a village near Alexandria where her father, Theon, was the local barber. Theon was also the local moneylender; he was of some minor repute in the vicinity, for his work on Geometric

Progression in Interest Calculations (used in a modified form to this day among credit card issuers). Hypatia's early years are a complete mystery. After mention of her birth, the next reference we have is of her admission to the Second Alexandrian School. We don't know the circumstances under which she secured her admission, though we know it was very rare for a woman to pursue tertiary education in those times. Her first two years at the school were uneventful. The typical course consisted of two sections. Theoretical studies included Euclidian geometry, astronomy, philosophy, war mechanics, and triangulation among other subjects. Practical studies included courses on bread and wine making, mixing of flour, kneading, grinding, charm and etiquette. Test results show her as a gifted student with high scores in most subjects, except grinding. She was not a good grinder, and the flour ratios she used for making pasta dough were more suited for vermicelli.

It was during the third year, by when she had resigned herself to a lifetime of vermicelli, that she postulated her famous theorem on the Vanishing Unit, known today as the Hypatian Theorem. It was a return to abstraction in mathematical terms and bordered on philosophical enquiry.

Expressed mathematically, it stated:

Economic Unit Given = Economic Unit Received - Hypatia Constant

i.e. Economic unit received is the sum of Economic Unit given less Hypatia Constant

The Hypatia Constant (the existence is a constant, not the magnitude) is a variable. The magnitude is unknown and varies for individual instances, but the equation is always the same. The sum total on both sides is always equal and it is always an addition function. The Economic Unit could be currency, gold, wheat or chickens, but never sheep. Professor Holmes used a famous observation to explain the Hypatia Constant. Assume the government allotted USD 100 to a farmer. The farmer will always receive less than USD 100 due to the existence of the Hypatia constant. The farmer might get USD 10 or USD 99 in hand. But never the full USD 100. The remaining USD 90 vanishes. Where the money disappears can never be ascertained, even with the latest forensic knowledge.

It should be noted that Hypatia never used the word 'Constant' and instead chose to call it the Vanishing Unit. Later day, mathematicians have compacted it to the Hypatia Constant. The impact of her postulation on the Alexandrian populace was tremendous, since, with a simple theorem she explained the disappearance of millions of gold talents from the treasury. It satisfied the treasury officials, the nobility and the citizens as it identified the location of all the missing gold. It vanishes, and as the theorem postulates, it can never be ascertained. All were able to sleep better knowing that the location can never be determined. The enrollment in the auditing profession has shot up due to the removal of the responsibility of finding the missing money.

Professor Holmes in his Miami lectures (or as a lecher in Miami; the note was unclear) highlighted the connection between the Hypatian Theorem and the Heisenberg's uncertainty principle. While the uncertainty principle was applicable to the atomic world, specifically the electron, Hypatian theorem is specifically about government grants and subsidies. A recent case involving a major pharmaceutical company indicates its timelessness and universal applicability.

The circumstance surrounding her death has mainly been gleaned from few references in Diophantus's Porisms. While Diophantus's work is primarily on the cube and its relations to spheres, he is better known for the few glimpses he has provided into Hypatia's life. Professor Holmes has based his study mainly on Diophantus's treatise and Fibonacci's Liber Abaci. While Professor Holmes was not proficient in Greek or Latin, this has not hampered him. Where he couldn't comprehend the texts, which was most of it, he has used his imagination. Using a strong white light and the intuition deductive methodology that he was famous for, Professor Holmes has managed to stitch together the life of Hypatia, or to be more precise, the death of Hypatia. However, in his Miami lecture, he admitted that most of his conclusions are unsubstantiated. Hypatia was murdered, possibly in her sleep. Was she alone at the time is not known. Her lack of proficiency in grinding (the flour) would point to a solitary death. Instigators, possibly were the treasury officials. While the initial response to her observation was warm, over a period of time, it led to a diminishing of all economic unit activity. The magnitude of the Hypatia constant started increasing, leading to unit activity approaching zero.

i.e. lim HC = o~o

EUR - > 0

Some economists and mathematicians have put an alternate interpretation forward. Refer note ‡ for further details. This led to a period of social unrest among the people. Unemployment, initially, in double digits progressed to triple digits. The unemployed became more than the total work force (due to multitasking workers). Manufacturing and services sector, except retailing, saw a drop in turnover. Retailing continued to prosper, but without any products, eventually started selling the empty space on their racks (an early example of product placement). The farming sector, deemed unfashionable, was the most severely impacted. The cows stopped producing milk. Soon the bulls followed.

The financial and credit markets collapsed. Fed officials soon realised that with the 'HC' (Hypatia Constant) approaching infinity, there was no need, for actual provision or granting of Economic Unit. They could eliminate the middleman i.e. the recipient altogether. The government grants went directly into their pockets, thus eliminating all kinds of paperwork. The more enlightened of the divisional heads further deduced that they could eliminate the middle management too, thus reducing costs further.

The Alexandrian stock exchange collapsed. Daily trade dropped by 60% and market capitalisation sunk by 80%. The Nice Donkey

Company, a major transportation services company and a bell weather of the exchange, went under. The donkeys were laid off without warning. The much awaited Alexandrian Power Company's IPO was undersubscribed and the subscription guarantees had to be invoked.

The people (and the donkeys) blamed Hypatia for their misery. The Second Alexandrian School came under a cloud of suspicion. There were demands for disbanding and nationalising the school. The people screamed. The donkeys and the politicians brayed. The people wanted retribution. The government's investigative department, Office of Serious Fraud, refused to take action till Hypatia publicly confessed to the fraud. She was branded a subversive and her vermicelli was confiscated. Her health started failing. She vainly tried to make pasta, but at the time of her greatest need, she couldn't remember the ratios for making the dough; and it turned to vermicelli. It too was confiscated.

Disgraced and hungry, she went to bed, clutching the first edition papyrus of her theorems. The next day, her body was found with a knife pierced in her heart. The papyrus was never found. She was cremated and her ashes were buried. With her death, the Second School went into a decline. Her contemporaries like Thymaridas, Nicomachus and Pappus migrated to Constantinople and started the Byzantine school.

The Alexandrian School received multiple bailouts, got nationalised and eventually became the Alexandrian Insurance Group (AIG).

‡ **Note:**

lim HC = o~o

EUR - > 0

Some economists have provided an alternate interpretation i.e. the Hungarian Cents tends to approach infinity as the Euro approaches zero. Would this be mathematically possible? The closest a currency has been able to approach infinity has been the Zimbabwean Dollar. This has led to everyone becoming a multi-millionaire overnight. Labour shortages and extinction of all manufacturing activity has ensued. It seems to reflect the Alexandrian experience.

Chapter Eight
La Carjavalian Science

It started with the pigeons. The reader would have noticed by now an inherent vanity in Professor Holmes. He wanted to be remembered. He wanted to be the giant that others could stand on. He venerated science but was afraid of the gods. His mantle had two triumvirates. One had Charles Darwin, Isaac Newton and Leo Szilard (one explained man's journey, the other taught us to calculate man's journey, and the last provided us with atomic clues to end man's journey). The other triumvirate on a much less visible mantle was the Father, the Son and the Holy Ghost. Depending on the vagaries of his fortune, his prayers shifted between the two.

He wanted to explain the Iberian lack of pigeons in evolutionary terms. Like Darwin, he knew this could be his 'Galapagos Island'. He didn't believe in the Carjavalian effect (refer Cocoa Forever for an explanation) and suspected the existence of a more evolutionary answer. It could be the flora of the region. Perhaps it was the wind patterns or the region's magnetic compass inhibiting the migrations. He knew he had to start by studying the arboreal habitats in Ibercia, but it required a visit to the region.

His meagre financial resources did not easily permit such a venture. His consultancy works for the industrialists were drying up with the green movement. There were few verdant forests left to raze. His salary was not enough for both the tickets and the accommodation. He could afford only one of the two: the stay or the tickets. He evaluated buying the ticket without actual travelling, but realised its futility. He then evaluated staying in Iberia, but without any mode of reaching there it was pointless. He finally decided to stay where he was (an outcome familiar to many of us who have faced such predicaments).

His tenacity led him to find alternative sources of research material. He wrote to the Iberian Tourism Board for material on the flora and fauna of the region. They were delighted to receive his letter. This was the first time anyone had written to them. This was the first time anyone had wanted to visit Iberia. The envelope was leaked to the press. The whole country was overjoyed. There were celebrations and parades planned. Finally good sense prevailed and it was decided to read the letter. There was gloom, when they realised he was not visiting Iberia. The celebrations and parades were cancelled. Their reply was curt. They referred him to the Iberian Wild Ministry (Iberian Wildlife Ministry: absence of a life there led to its shortening to 'Wild').

Though disconcerted at their terse reply, he remained tenacious. He wrote to the Iberian Wild Ministry. The country was overjoyed again. This was the second letter Iberia had received in a matter of few weeks. Finally, the world was noticing them. They made plans to ask for a permanent seat in the Security Council.

The Wild Minister ordered copies of all geological and cartographical maps to be sent to Professor Holmes. They didn't have any. Finally a clerk from the Iberian Tourism Board was deputed to travel around the countryside and take pictures. These pictures were sent to Professor Holmes. Seeing the pictures, Professor Holmes realised the enormity of the task. He was trying to establish an avian evolutionary fork, based on random non-serial grainy photographs. He decided it was futile to continue with this line of study. As he had already started his research work, he shifted his focus to studying La Carjaval.

La Carjaval was a fascinating but unsung hero of science. He was more known for his treatment of the New World inhabitants and his mistreatment of the pigeons. He was gentle with the Aztecs and cruel to the pigeons. He pillaged and plundered politely. He raped with consideration. The Aztec women adored him. The pigeons were afraid of him. But it his science, that Professor Holmes was interested in.

La Carjaval's work spanned optics, trigonometry and triangulation methods. His profession as a soldier triggered his interest in this aspect of science. His interest in optics started very early. He couldn't sight his musket due to insufficient light. He realised that lighting was the key to a successful shot. He conceived the differences in sensitivity of the human eye. He identified the different wavelengths for cones and rods. He may be the father of photometry (DNA results are inconclusive).

His greatest contribution to the field of optics was the Carjavalian Luminous Scale. He quantified the scale using simple words and demonstrated the effectiveness by shooting simple people.

Scale Value	Time	Description	Effect on Simple People
CLS 1	10 AM TO 3 PM	Strong Light	Clean shot. Instant death.
CLS 2	8-10 AM & 3-5 PM	Medium Light	Good shot. Might die.
CLS 3	6-8 AM & 5-6 PM	Low Light	Bad shot. Probably hit the leg.
CLS 4	5-6 AM & 6-7 PM	Dim Light	Very Bad shot. Miracle Level
CLS 5	7PM TO 5 AM	No Light	Impossible. Only if the simple person ran towards the gun.

He was a diligent and careful experimenter. He conducted all the measurements at zero altitude, at equator on summer solstice. He started with volunteers. At various times of the day, the volunteers were subjected to being shot. When volunteers were unavailable, which was almost immediately, he used prisoners. He measured their reactions, wherever proffered. The silent and unconscious ones were grouped under CLS 5.

Having thus established the basic principles of lighting and lapidation, La Carjaval turned to triangulation. At that time, the muzzle velocities possible using basic chemicals were minimal and entirely in the subsonic range. It was a function of the quantity of the propellant used. Quite often, the bullet or the missile would fall half way to the target, dragged down by wind resistance and gravity.

This was an inefficient way of committing mayhem. La Carjaval decided to systemise the study of rocketry. Firstly, he had to develop a system for determining the target. His superiors usually communicated this. He tried to change this downward flow of communication by ordering his superiors, but the experiment backfired. On threat of court martial and hanging, he quickly gave up this line of research. Then he had to develop a way to measure the distance to the target. With immobile surfaces like buildings and forts this was simple using the *sinucidere methodi*.

With a moving target it was cumbersome to move the muzzle and the triangulation equipment. He overcame this by usually requesting his enemies to flee in a straight line. With the co-operation of his enemies, he went to work on designing the cross-staff. He also designed the modern semi-circle protractor. To determine the degrees, he used 180 workers standing in a semi-circle with arms outstretched. He couldn't complete the full-circle protractor due to paucity of workers. He was also one of the first to propose using two telescopes in a perpendicular axis to study the celestial bodies (using one telescope to study earthly bodies was already discovered and very popular in his time). As it so often happens, his mathematical accomplishments were overshadowed by his nefarious reputation. Had he, in his later years, renounced his enmity and made peace with pigeons, it might have helped him in consolidating his theoretical work and getting the attention he deserved. He had laid the framework for long distance warfare. He could be called the grandfather of rocketry.

Professor Holmes's research paper on La Carjaval was never published. The university deemed it irrelevant. The military was interested and he was asked to make a presentation. Professor Holmes did not disclose any details because of the classified nature of the meeting. He did indicate that the military requires volunteers to fine-tune the Carjavalian Luminous Scale to suit local conditions.

‡ **Note:**

The sinucidere method involved using an unwilling volunteer, if a willing moron was not available, to count the paces loudly, as he walked towards the fort or the enemy. Few made it all the way. If anyone reached the fort it was a perfecto calculatio. Else, the rest of the distance was roughly estimated and added to the final numeric utterance of the volunteer.

Chapter Nine
Dahoneyan, The Goddess of Love

Professor Holmes was unsuccessful in love. He was unsuccessful in his attempt at marriage. In love, and by extension, he hoped, in marriage, his ideal was his village chief's daughter. She had (and presumably still has) long thick black hair, which reached her hips and long thick legs that reached the ground. While he found many similarly gifted women in the campus; unfortunately, none graced his classes. It seemed to him that his adopted vocation of archaeology was bereft of specimens with these endowments. But he realised that he was better off than the particle physics department, his original choice of a vocation.

In marriage, he stuck to his derived formula (refer to Bride's Worth for the detailed calculations). The fractional requirement was not conducive to his search. He experimented with introducing various levels of confidence into his calculations. However, the results still varied from 7.4 to 7.8. Whole numbers still eluded him. He was willing to compromise on his ideal and frequently forayed into the arts department in search of suitable brides. This did not go well with his colleagues in the Particle Physics department, as they were on a similar quest, though they were using string theory as foundation (with little success since it varied from 11 to 13).

The physicists demanded equal visitation rights, using strings as their argument. The dispute eventually died with Professor Holmes's retreating. Thus, he (and the particle physicists) started to contemplate an unmarried life. While this suited him, his libido and ardour were not cooperating. He contemplated procuring a dog, but his libido disagreed. His ardour was more reasonable and willing to compromise. They suggested sheep but campus rules prohibited grazing animals. Despondent, angry and in constant conflict with his libido, he decided to abandon the mathematical method and try more mystical options.

Due to his fame in his field, he had many foreign students in his course. One of them was, Felix Esperanto, an exchange student from Caribbean (it is not clear what he was exchanged for). Felix suggested praying to Dahoneyan, their goddess of love. She was the patron saint of the unmarried, the ones with little prospects of marriage and the married, who wished they were unmarried. To understand this poignant, bitter and ultimately unfulfilled quest, we have to understand Dahoneyan and her cult. To the serious scholar, it provides clues to his subsequent conversion and adoption of a pure dianoetic way of thinking. To the more phronemophobic and prurient scholars, it is a good romantic story.

Dahoneyan was a very insatiable god as befitting her specialty; she required elaborate rituals to please her. While jealousy seems to have been a common divine trait, some openly stated, others through deduction, Dahoneyan was an especially jealous god. Her story is full of contradictions, and serious historians ridicule the cult in public. In private, they worship her fervently.

Dahoneyan had become a love goddess not out of choice. She had been, in what is euphemistically called, a comely girl. She had been a happy child growing up, spending most of her time on the seashore, collecting seashells and coconuts, and doing other things comely girls do. With the seashells, she made elaborate and intricate necklaces that she sold to the tourists.

Since this happened in the 17th century, historians often quote this as an incongruity. Tourism was non-existent, unless the infrequent transatlantic pirate ship and its involuntary hostages, were considered tourists. If she did have contact with them, it is unlikely that she would not have been asked to join the cruise. Unless she was really, really comely!

Her father, as told and pointed out to her by her mother, (they practiced polyandry) was the village's grocer. Since very little cultivation was possible in the sandy atoll, he mainly sold coconuts. The grocery was not a very profitable enterprise. The main medium of exchange or currency, besides simple bartering and thieving, was the coconut. Everyone and everything was paid with coconuts.

Initially, the villagers paid her father with a coconut, for every coconut they purchased. Soon they realised, they already had a coconut to begin with, and stopped purchasing at the grocery. Sometimes when the coconut money was of a higher denomination, he had to give change and since coconut was usually indivisible, he had to pay two coconuts. Despite these setbacks, her father persevered. He was a kind man. He loved to play with her and would frequently help her in making the necklaces.

When she was around ten and approaching the marriageable age, her mother started looking for a boy. Given her comeliness, it was generally felt that more distant atolls, out of visual range, would be a better suited for a bridegroom. Many smoke signals were passed between the islands and few proposals were received. Since it was customary for the girl to meet the boy before matrimony, she had to undertake frequent visits to the neighbouring islands. The journeys were perilous, since as a girl, she was forbidden from using the canoes. She was usually wrapped in coconut husks (for floatation) and put to sea. The village elders studied the stars and the tides, and suggested the direction and time she was to be launched.

Many a night was spent drifting in the sea, praying for the veracity of the elder's calculations, mixed with eager anticipation. Occasionally she would drift to other islands. The islanders being kind, would ascertain the reason for her visit, feed her, and then propel her in the general direction of the potential groom's island.

She passed a couple of months like this in the sea, visiting different islands. She met many boys during these journeys. While she was treated well everywhere, the dearth of her practical skills coupled with comeliness proved to be a hindrance. She demonstrated her necklace making skills. She would make one and offer it to the boy's family. They mostly congratulated her and then threw it away.

Eventually, tired and heart broken she decided to return to her own island. On her way back, in the middle of the sea, dejected and angry with all the islanders and their lack of appreciation for her charms, she took a mighty vow.

In a thunderous voice, she said: "Oh God, the all knowing Coconut God, the one who makes the trees, the sand, the sweet nectar of the unripe coconut, who blows the breeze in the warm afternoon, Why have you cursed me? Have I not been devoted to you? Have I not walked on the same sand? From this moment, I renounce ALL coconuts and ALL men. I shall not partake of either. I shall remain celibate."

It is said that, when she took the oath, the sky became dark; the seas became angry, the waters churned and frothed, the fish and other oceanic creatures stood still. After some time everything returned to normal. The heavens cleared, the sea became more amiable, the water stopped churning, and adopted its usual wavy pattern; and the fish stopped being still. We do not know what happened to the other oceanic creatures. Presumably, they too moved on. But not all!

Suddenly, out of the oceanic depths, rose a giant beast. Half Fish, Half Lion and Half Woman! It was covered in gold interspersed with blue shiny circles made of pearls. It was very wet. Its face was that of a beautiful woman, but with a gleaming leonine mane (possibly a very hirsute woman). The beast thundered: "Oh Dahoneyan! You are so young and you are so prett... Ummm... you are so young! Why have you taken this vow? Do you know what it means? A life without Coconuts!"

Dahoneyan replied: "Oh... Oh... Who are you?

The beast answered: "I am Maryanethra, the wife of the Coconut God. I beseech you to take back your oath. A life without the its juicy nectar is no life at all. I am saying from personal experience, since I have not tasted it for a long, long time."

But, Dahoneyan could not be dissuaded. Finally, exasperated, but with admiration, Maryanethra thundered: "Dahoneyan, you are a foolish but passionate young woman. As you wished, you shall remain celibate, loveless and coconut-less. You will be the patron of the unloved men, women and coconuts. They will worship you, and you in your divine, but foolish kindness, bring Love to their barren and thirsty hearts. Their hearts will flutter, and thus fluttered, will bow to their destiny. You will bring fantasy and desire and in case of men, tumescence, to their empty and flaccid lives. But you will not bestow your favours easily. The devotee must prove himself worthy of the Love."

Modern readers will notice what is popularly know as the disclaimer clause or fine print in Maryanethra's benediction. Due to the polysemous last line, devotion to Dahoneyan and its associated rituals have varied between the islands. There were, and are, different ways to get Dahoneyan blessings. But all require a complete absence of coconuts in their diet.

The reader, would have by now, understood the arduous and painful sacrifices that Dahoneyan demanded for her favours. For Professor Holmes, who was fond of coconuts, these restrictions were, to say the least, painful. But he persevered. Professor Holmes, along with an excited Felix flew to the Caribbean. His finances did not permit a room in the hotel. Luckily, Felix, understanding his situation offered him the use of his ancestral hut. The hut was rudimentary, but had been in his family for many generations. It consisted of four bamboo pillars, set in the sand, covered with a bluish-grey tarpaulin. Felix's grandfather, in keeping with the modern times, had reluctantly agreed to the tarpaulin. His grandfather welcomed Professor Holmes warmly. His bags were taken, three of the youngest children were kicked out, and the vacant space so created was given to Professor Holmes.

He found his reputation had preceded him. Everyone knew of his work. They met the local witch doctor and explained the situation. The doctor was more interested in the formula worked out by Professor

Holmes. He agreed that fractions could be a hindrance and might interfere in proper consummation of the marriage. But he tried to talk Professor Holmes out of seeking Dahoneyan's help. He knew the rigours of that path.

He suggested using an incomplete woman, perhaps with an extremity missing. He would still have the use of the remaining 7.6th of the woman. The lack of the balance 0.4th part would not be usually very noticeable, adding, that he knew many women who he felt, were not entirely complete. Professor Holmes explained that this was a distortion of his original formula and declined to accept this reasoning. Finally, it was decided to proceed with the supplication and the material for the ceremony was requisitioned. Fourteen chickens of a comely appearance, signifying the 14 islands Dahoneyan visited on her quest, were procured. All the villagers from these 14 islands were invited. Almost all came.

The ceremony started. Professor Holmes was asked to shout Dahoneyan's name thrice. Then the first chicken was beheaded and the blood poured over Professor Holmes's head, indicating the redemption of his brain. The second chicken's blood was poured over his eyes, thus delivering his sight from narrow and limited visual desires. The third was splashed on his nose, remitting him of unwanted olfactory preferences. The next five were poured on his heart, signifying his escape from strong desires.

By this time, the professor had absolutely no desires. He was willing to marry anyone, of female gender. Black hair and thick legs seemed frivolous at this point. But there were another six more to go. The next five were spilled on his groin denoting complete freedom in his discernment. The prayers were beginning to be answered. At this point in the ceremony, Professor Holmes was willing to consummate with any vertebrate. It didn't need to be even animated. The last and final chicken was released, to mark the free spirit of the love goddess. Professor Holmes tried to catch it; it being a vertebrate; but he was unsuccessful.

Next day, it was generally felt that the commune was a great success. Professor Holmes felt the same. He felt lusty. He had no taste, and was very egalitarian in his selection as long as it was feminine. Many women from the village visited him. They left satisfied, and some of them left with more than satisfaction. The chickens gave him a wide berth. Professor Holmes did not want to leave this idyllic and verdant island full of lascivious possibilities. But duty called, and as we have seen, Professor Holmes was very dutiful. He was full of duty.

Felix and he returned. Felix left the university almost immediately. He started a 'Dahoneyan' tour to the island with remarkable success. Professor Holmes continued to indulge in his indiscriminate pursuits. Nobody was safe.

Chapter Ten
A Reluctant Candidate

Professor Holmes did not want to stand for the election. He did it for 'security'. Not his, but the university's. Unlike many other phenomena that falls under this umbrella in our country like small time politicians, UFOs, missile testing and airport checks, Holmes's reasons were very genuine. A spate of burglaries and attacks inside the campus had led to a fearful environment. The classes were getting affected. The experiments were going awry. The university council had deliberated recruiting security guards, but embezzlement and larceny had drained the available resources. In fact, with the current cost of living, the council was unsure whether, what was left would be enough for future peculation.

With no help forthcoming, each department was left to fend for itself. As head of the department, Professor Holmes was in a difficult situation. The department library contained many priceless texts and artefacts. At the department meeting, the professors fearlessly and unselfishly, volunteered the services of the students for guard duties. However, the student's watch did not reduce the incidence of attacks. They, being archaeology students, and used to peering at minute objects in the ground, were unused to a more upright and horizontal line of sight required for catching thieves. They did, though manage to stop a large number of crawling insects from entering the building.

After a week of various tribulations, all he was left with was a rampaging band of archaeology students, decimating the insect and rodent populations within the campus. After strong protests from the biology department, he was reluctantly forced to stop the massacre.

It was around this time that the general elections were announced. The whole country was getting ready for the 'Great Game' and newspapers carried only news on politics and politicians. One thing all the politicians had in common was security cover. They were secure.

Men with guns, dark sunglasses and suits surrounded them. The security levels varied from a single man to groups of men. This clinched his inner turmoil and he decided to get himself elected. At the least he would get one man and it was infinitely better than the lethal and murderous bunch of student insect killers, he had currently.

Now he needed to figure out on how to get elected. He did intensive research on the 'Great Game' and arrived at a few key requirements to win. As usual, he had made copious notes and I have been lucky to find them. I have reproduced them below verbatim. For easier comprehension, I have added clarifications in italics below his notes.

Win Election... To be Candidate... Minimum Requirements...

a) family name... important to have a family name...else could be mistaken for a person without a family!

Notes: What Holmes means is having a famous family name. This usually helps in getting the requisite funding and more importantly a ticket to run for the election. Holmes had considered changing his name but had found the process cumbersome. Next he considered joining a famous family but realised that he could do so only through marriage or adoption. With Dahoneyan's blessing, he had a fecund circle of friends to prove his virility and did not want to restrict his prowess to a single woman through marriage. That left, only, adoption. Accordingly, he had tried to get himself adopted by the various rich families, but with no success. It seemed they all had numerous and unwanted children, of their own and some of them offered Professor Holmes a few in return for adoption.

b) war record... seems to be a basic requirement... all have it... but how to get one? Are there exams for getting one...and if so, who and what frequency is it conducted? What area should I get one? The options are endless...

Notes: I know the Professor was willing to get a war record. He pondered endlessly on fighting but he found assault distasteful. He finally gave up the idea when he realised it might involve physical work.

He tried to enlist but most of them rejected him. When he confessed his desire to join for political gains, they suggested he join the enemy's army. It would make their job easier.

c) social work... not feasible... I am what I am...

Notes: He tried to help the homeless, but he couldn't find one easily. When he did, most were suspicious of his attempts to help them.

d) Special status... religious or gender... or community!

Notes: He spent a lot of time trying to convert himself to a minority group. The minority groups were not amused and refused entrance.

e) Provide free food and alcohol or other forms of intoxicants... seems popular...

Notes: Professor Holmes had a lot of hope on this strategy. But he had badly misunderstood the practice and assumed that more he drank, more votes he would get. Therefore, he set himself a punishing routine of drinking. He drank from morning till evening, and after a one hour break continued the intake. Three days later he was admitted in a hospital with cirrhosis of the liver and a broken nose.

Fortunately, Professor Holmes had to spend only a week at the hospital. The liver though greatly stressed had recovered from the great alcoholic deluge, and the nose was beginning to fuse itself to its remaining parts. By then the burglars, who had been vandalising and spreading fear in the campus, had been apprehended. The campus and the priceless texts and the artefacts were safe again. Only the insects were left with mortal worries. Professor Holmes was overjoyed on hearing the news. He realised he would not have won if he had contested. He just did not have any of the attributes that a successful candidate requires to play the 'Great Game'.

About the Author

Sanjay Panikar lives in Phoenix, Arizona with his wife. As a plodding government employee, he finds inspiration from the many colorful people he encounters. On the infrequent occasions his employer grants him a day off, he can be seen toiling in his shop doing 'Woodworking Projects'.

He can be contacted at sanjay.panikar@gmail.com.

Other Books by this Author

Please visit your favorite ebook retailer to discover other books by Sanjay Panikar:

- **Adventures of Subbu, the Baby Elephant**

www.ingramcontent.com/pod-product-compliance
Lightning Source LLC
Chambersburg PA
CBHW060504160726
47992CB00003B/1322